W9-AOP-128

ROCKFORD PUBLIC LIBRARY

3 1112 018293932

WITHDRAWN

E LEW
Lewis, J. Patrick
Tugg and Teeny : that's
what friends are for

022312

ROCKFORD PUBLIC LIBRARY

Rockford, Illinois

www.rockfordpubliclibrary.org

815-965-9511

WITHDRAWN

Tugg and Teeny

That's What Friends Are For

ROCKFORD PUBLIC LIBRARY

Written by J. Patrick Lewis

Illustrated by Christopher Denise

For Selis, with love, Grandpat

✩

For Asher and Erin, Chris

This book has a reading comprehension level of 2.7 under the ATOS®
readability formula. For information about ATOS please visit www.renlearn.com.
ATOS is a registered trademark of Renaissance Learning, Inc.

Lexile®, Lexile® Framework and the Lexile® logo are trademarks of MetaMetrics, Inc.,
and are registered in the United States and abroad. The trademarks and names of other
companies and products mentioned herein are the property of their respective owners.
Copyright © 2010 MetaMetrics, Inc. All rights reserved.

Text Copyright © 2012 J. Patrick Lewis
Illustration Copyright © 2012 Christopher Denise

All rights reserved. No part of this book may be reproduced in any manner
without the express written consent of the publisher, except in the case of brief
excerpts in critical reviews and articles. All inquiries should be addressed to:

Sleeping Bear Press™

315 E. Eisenhower Parkway, Suite 200
Ann Arbor, MI 48108
www.sleepingbearpress.com

Sleeping Bear Press is an imprint of Gale, a part of Cengage Learning.

10 9 8 7 6 5 4 3 2 1

Library of Congress Cataloging-in-Publication Data

Lewis, J. Patrick.
Tugg and Teeny : that's what friends are for / written by J. Patrick Lewis ;
illustrated by Christopher Denise.
v. cm.
Summary: Best friends Tugg, a gorilla, and Teeny, a monkey, find three
opportunities to be neighborly.
Contents: Margie Barge's tears — Rocko's horn — Good Neighbor Day.
ISBN 978-1-58536-516-6 (hardcover) — ISBN 978-1-58536-687-3 (pbk.)
[1. Neighborliness–Fiction. 2. Gorilla–Fiction. 3. Monkeys–Fiction.
4. Jungle animals–Fiction. 5. Best friends–Fiction. 6. Friendship–Fiction.] I. Denise,
Christopher, ill. II. Title. III. Title: Tugg and Teeny, that is what friends are for.
PZ7.L5866Tut 2012
[E]–dc22   2010053800

Printed by China Translation & Printing Services Limited, Guangdong Province,
China. Hardcover 1st printing/Softcover 1st printing. 10/2011

Table of Contents

Margie Barge's Tears

Teeny and Tugg ran through the jungle to join their friends for an early morning bath. But instead of being in the waterhole, everyone was standing around it. The water was full of air bubbles.

"Do you hear somebody crying, Tugg?"

Teeny asked.

Whooosh! Up out of the water burst

Margie Barge. She was blubbering big,

wet tears.

"What's the matter, Margie Barge?" asked

Tugg. "Are you hurt? Are you in pain?"

"Y-Yes and y-yes," she cried. "Just look at me, Tugg. Have you ever seen so many chins? I ate f-far too much g-grass and water plants, and now look at m-me!"

"Well, you are a hippo after all," said Teeny. "I thought hippos were happy being large."

"Do you know what 'hippopotamus' means?" Margie Barge asked. "It means 'river horse.' And that's me." She started to cry again.

Tugg had an idea. He whispered

something to Teeny, who scampered off

into the jungle.

"Well, Margie," said Tugg, "at least you do not have hair all over like me! No one can tell my front from my back!"

The other animals started to speak up.

Tina Hyena laughed loud and long. "Have you ever heard a laugh like that, Margie? It is so annoying that sometimes instead of laughing I feel like crying."

"Listen, Margie," said Barb Hedgehog.

"You should be glad you do not have prickles

like mine all over your body. Why, I even

scare Rory Lion!"

Margie Barge's smile was returning.

She did not feel quite so bad anymore.

Just then Teeny returned.

"Margie, meet Henry! He's new to the

neighborhood."

Henry took one look at Margie, then blinked as his skin turned pink. "Hello, gorgeous!" he said. "Who are you? The Queen of the Waterhole?"

"Well, I…" Now it was Margie's turn to blush.

"Wow!" said Henry. "Today must be my lucky day. Would you like to go for a swim?"

And Margie's tears went away for good.

As Tugg and Teeny walked home, the monkey said, "Margie Barge is hippy and happy again, Tuggboat."

"Yes, Monkeyface," said Tugg. "Thank goodness you were there to save the day."

Rocko's Horn

"Have you seen Rocko Rhino?" Teeny asked.

"No," said Tugg. "What is our good friend Rocko doing these days?"

Before Teeny could answer, Violet
jumped out of the jungle. The warthog was
out of breath. "Rocko lost his horn! Come
and see."

Teeny and Tugg and Violet ran all the
way to Rocko's house.

Poor Rocko was sitting in his backyard.

He did not look like the same Rocko at all.

"My horn is gone, Tugg! It was right here on my face," he cried. "It must have fallen off, but I do not know where it went. What good is a rhino without a horn? That is like a monkey without a tail!"

"Rocko," said Teeny. "I will find a substitute for your horn."

Tugg shook his head, but when Teeny made up her mind, nothing could stop her. She ran into the jungle to find a new horn.

Teeny stopped when she saw Cuddles Python eating a banana. *Perfect!* she thought. When she brought a banana back to Rocko, he strapped it on his head.

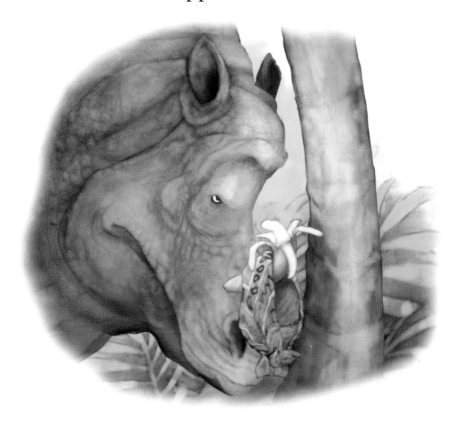

"No," said the rhino. "Too squishy."

Next, Teeny saw Margie Barge by the waterhole. She had a flower behind her ear. *That's it!* thought Teeny. But when the monkey tied the flower to Rocko's face, he sniffled, "*Achoo!*"

"No," said the rhino. "Too sneezy."

"Okay," said Teeny. "I have just the
thing—my music stick with the holes in it.
Will this work?" she asked.

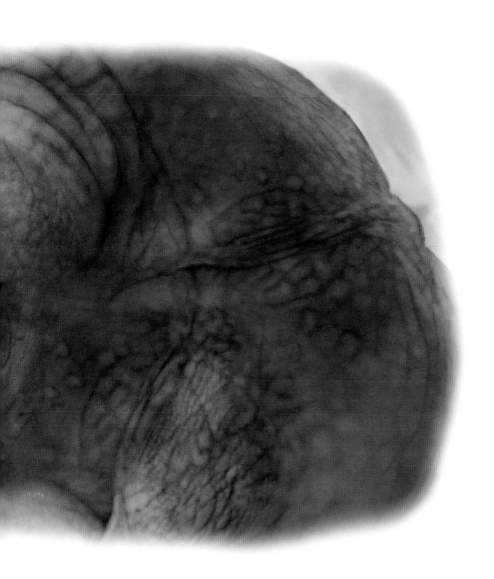

"No," said the rhino. "Too skinny."

He sat back down with a heavy thud.

All of a sudden, Tugg had an idea.

"How long have you been sitting here,

Rocko?" he asked.

"Three days," said the rhino. "Ever

since I lost my horn."

"Maybe if you stand back up and stretch, you will feel better."

"No, I am too sad," said Rocko.

"Will you please try?" asked Tugg.

"All right," sighed Rocko.

Rocko stood up on his four legs. He stretched. He looked to the right. He looked to the left. Then he looked at where he had been sitting. There was his horn. He had been sitting on it the whole time.

"Sometimes the answer is as plain

as the nose on your face," said Tugg. "And

sometimes your horn is right under

your nose."

Good Neighbor Day

The day was almost done in Sidekick Thicket, and Tugg and Teeny had just finished giving their house a new coat of paint.

"Guess what tomorrow is, Teeny," said Tugg.

"The weekend, thank goodness," said the monkey. "I am pooped."

"No, not that. Tomorrow is Good Neighbor Day."

"What is that?" asked Teeny.

"Well, to show that we are good neighbors," said Tugg, "we will invite all of our friends over for a picnic. Everyone brings a favorite dish. It's called a potluck."

"Then we have finished painting just in time," said Teeny, smiling.

"One more thing, Teeny," said Tugg.

"Please paint the picnic table bench but

be quick about it. I'll go tell all our friends

while you are finishing up."

But Teeny thought to herself,

Sometimes monkeys just need to rest.

So she took out her notepad and

began to write a poem—

"Housepainting = Hard

Work."

Then she practiced

playing a song on her music

stick—"Ooga-Chaca-

Ooga-Ooga-Ooga-

Chaca."

Next she painted a picture on her easel—*A Rose for a Gorilla.*

So it was quite late by the time Teeny finally got around to painting the picnic bench.

The next day friends from all over the jungle arrived for the potluck.

Flap the Elephant said, "Love the new paint job, Tugg. Your house sparkles!"

"Yes, it does, and what a beautiful shade of violet," said Violet.

"Thank you," said Tugg and Teeny.

Everything looked and smelled so tasty.

"Happy Good Neighbor Day to one and

all!" Tugg said. "Let the potluck begin!"

And so it did.

But after they had eaten, and the

guests got up to leave, Teeny nearly fainted.

Everyone had a big violet stripe on his or

her bottom!

"Oh no!" Teeny whispered. "Look,

Tugg! The paint on the bench did not dry."

What a mess! Tugg thought.

Thinking quickly, Tugg said, "Dear friends, we wanted this to be a day to remember. So Teeny and I decided to give each of you a special gift. Please look behind you. It is your very own tattoo."

The animals stared at each others'

backsides in silence. Then …

Rory Lion roared, "*Grooovy!*"

Tina Hyena laughed, "*Sweeeet!*"

And everyone hooted and hollered all

the way home.

Later that night, when the guests were gone, Teeny said, "I waited too long to paint the picnic bench, didn't I, Tuggboat?"

"Yes, you did, Monkeyface," said Tugg, "but everyone had fun at the picnic, and thanks to you, they went home with a pretty painting that they will enjoy for a very long time."